Rumblewick's ~~My~~ DIARY

My Unwilling Witch Gets a Makeover

Hiawyn Oram • Sarah Warburton

L B

LITTLE, BROWN AND COMPANY

New York Boston

To my sister, who knows all about making-over
H.O.

For Jasmine
S.W.

Text copyright © 2007 by Hiawyn Oram
Illustrations copyright © 2007 by Sarah Warburton

Little, Brown and Company

Hachette Book Group
237 Park Avenue, New York, NY 10017
Visit our website at www.lb-kids.com

Little, Brown and Company is a division of Hachette Book Group,
Inc. The Little, Brown name and logo are trademarks of Hachette Book Group, Inc.

First U.S. Edition: February 2010
First published in Great Britain in 2007 by Orchard Books

Library of Congress Cataloging-in-Publication Data

Oram, Hiawyn.
My unwilling witch gets a makeover / by Hiawyn Oram ; illustrated by Sarah Warburton.
—1st U.S. ed.
p. cm. — (Rumblewick's diary ; #4)
Summary: Rumblewick, a Highly Qualified Witch's Cat, records in his diary what happens
when his reluctant young witch tries to pursue a modeling career on the Other Side.
ISBN 978-0-316-03462-3
[I. Witches—Fiction. 2. Cats—Fiction. 3. Beauty culture—Fiction. 4. Diaries—Fiction.
5. Humorous stories.] I. Warburton, Sarah, ill. II. Title.
PZ7.0624Mp 2009
[Fic]—dc22

2009000204

10 9 8 7 6 5 4 3 2 1

RRD-C

Printed in the United States of America

CONTRACT OF SERVICE

between
WITCH HAGATHA AGATHA, Haggy Aggy for short, HA for shortest
of Thirteen Chimneys, Wizton-under-Wold
&
the Witch's Familiar,
RUMBLEWICK SPELLWACKER MORTIMER B, RB for short

It is hereby agreed that, come
FIRE, Brimstone, CAULDRONS overflowing,
or ALIEN WIZARDS invading,
for the NEXT SEVEN YEARS
RB will serve HA,
obey her EVERY WHIM AND WORD and at all times assist her
in the ways of being a true and proper WITCH.

PAYMENT for services will be:
* a log basket to sleep in * unlimited slime buns for breakfast
* free use of HA's broomsticks (outside of peak brooming hours)
* and a cracked mirror for luck.

PENALTY for failing in his duties will be decided on the whim of
THE HAGS ON HIGH.

SIGNED AND SEALED
this New Moon Day, 22nd of Remember

Haggy Aggy
....
Witch Hagatha Agatha

Rumblewick
Rumblewick Spellwacker Mortimer B

Trixie Fiddlestick
And witnessed by the High Hag Trixie Fiddlestick

A SHORT HISTORY
OF HOW YOU COME TO BE READING MY
VERY PRIVATE DIARIES

In a snail shell, they were STOLEN. Oh yes, no less. My witch, Haggy Aggy (HA for short), sneaked into my log basket and helped herself.

According to her, this is what happened:

On one of her many shopping trips to Your Side she met a Book Wiz. (I am told you call them publishers, though Wiz seems more fitting as they make books appear, as if by magic, every day of the week.)

Anyway, this Book Wiz/publisher wanted HA to write an account of HER life as a witch here on Our Side. Of course, HA wasn't willing to do that. Being the most unwilling witch in witchdom, she is far too busy shopping, watching TV, not cackling, being anything BUT a witch, and getting me into trouble with the High Hags* as a result.

The Book Wiz begged on her knees (apparently) and offered HA a life's supply of shoes if she came up with something. So HA did. She came up with THIS — MY DIARIES. ALL OF THEM!!!!

Of course, when I wrote the diaries, I was not expecting anyone to read them. Let alone Othersiders like you. But as you are, here is a word to the wise about how things work between us:

---

* The High Hags run everything around here. They RULE.

1. We are here on THIS SIDE and you are there on the OTHER SIDE.

2. Between us is the HORIZON LINE.

3. You don't see we're here, on This Side, living our lives, because for you the Horizon Line is <u>always a day away</u>. You can walk for a thousand moons (or more for all I know), but you'll never reach it.

4. On the other paw, we know you're there because we visit you all the time. This is partly because of broomsticks. A broomstick has no trouble with any Horizon Line anywhere. A broomstick (with one or more of us upon it) just flies straight through.

And it has to be like that because scaring Otherside children into their wits is part of witches' work. In fact it is Number One on the Witches' Charter of Good Practice (see copy glued at the back).

On the other paw, it is NOWHERE in the Charter for a witch to go over to Your Side to make friends and try to be and do everything you are and do — <u>as my witch</u>, Haggy <u>Aggy, does</u>.

But then, that's my giant problem: being cat to a witch who doesn't want to be one. And as you will see from these diaries, it makes my life a right BAG OF HEDGEHOGS. So all I can say is, if HA tries to make friends with YOU, send her straight back to This Side with a spider in her ear.

Thank you,
Rumblewick *Spellwacker Mortimer B.* xxx

This Diary Belongs to:

Rumblewick Spellwacker Mortimer B.

RUMBLEWICK for short, RB for shortest

Address:
Thirteen Chimneys,
Wizton-under-Wold, This Side
Bird's Eye View: 331 N by WW

Telephone:
77+3-5+1-7

Nearest Otherside Telephone:
Ditch and Candleberry Bush Street,
N by SE Over the Horizon

Birthday:
Windy Day 23rd Magogary

EDUCATION:
The Awethunder School for Familiars
12-Moon Apprenticeship to the
High Hag Witch Trixie Fiddlestick

QUALIFICATIONS:
Certified Witch's Familiar

CURRENT EMPLOYMENT:
Seven-year contract with Witch Hagatha Agatha,
Haggy Aggy for short, HA for shortest

HOBBIES:
Cathastics, Point-to-Point Shrewing, Languages

NEXT OF KIN:
Uncle Sherbet (retired Witch's Familiar)
Moldy Old Cottage,
Flying Teapot Street,
Prancetown

Dear Diary,

Haggy Aggy has gone to Witch Rattle's for a Bad Temper Competition — giving me a chance to catch up on a few things of my own.

The good news is this: there's only one night to go till Fright Night — and I can hardly wait!!

Probably you don't know about Fright Night (how would you; you're a diary), so I'll tell you.

Fright Night is the night we dress up as ghastly ghouly characters like witch-hunters and vampire dogs and gather in the Narrow Avoid to celebrate who we are by trying to scare each other witless!

The witch and her Familiar who scare the most of us — by dawn — win.

Then — when the High Hags have counted up the scores, their Familiars have served us hot comfrey tea, and our wits have returned — we fly back to the Hags' Headquarters. There the Hags present the trophy to the winners in a supernova ceremony with shooting stars and a bonfire of old broomsticks. It truly is the best night ever.

I'm hoping to go as a Giant Witch-Eating Tarantula and my costume is spelled up, ready, and impatient. But so far HA is saying she thinks she'll give the whole thing a miss. Give Fright Night a miss? I ask you: what kind of a witch gives Fright Night a miss?

(Answer: only mine, dear Diary, only mine!)

TADPOLES
IN SOCKS!

What's THAT hurtling down the garden
path in a cloud of pink? Looks like HA.
Better go and see what THIS is all about.

Dear Diary,

The hurtling cloud was her. As it turns out, she hasn't been near Witch Rattle's Bad Temper Competition. ("Oh, RB," she defended herself, "why should I? I always win. Witch Rattle and her friends wouldn't know a Bad Temper if it knocked them off their broomsticks.")

Instead, she's been shopping on the Other Side. And I'm sorry to say, but this is what she's been shopping for:

ROSE, PEACH, GERANIUM, CARNATION,

PALE, SHOCKING, TOADSTOOL,

PENICILLIN, CAT'S TONGUE,

BAT'S TONGUE — whatever — PINK.

Skirts, tiddly tops, dresses, stockings, petticoats, hats, shoes, buckles, bangles, and neckwear —

ALL IN PINK!

She's already packed all her black into her flying trunk and made me send it to the broomstick shed.

"OUT OF MY SIGHT, RB!"

she said.

"BLACK IS YESTERDAY.

PINK IS THE NEW BLACK!"

I tried to reason with her. "But witches wear black," I said. "It's what they do. It's UNIFORM. There's never been a witch in witchdom in top-to-toe pink."

"Well, why not?" she said. "What's wrong with a witch in pink? I adore pink."

With that she opened a box of cocoalots topped with PINK sugar roses she'd bought on her PINK shopping spree, turned on Otherside TV, and flung herself onto the sofa like a giant pink powder puff.

I pushed a cup of comfrey tea and a slime bun in front of her — in the midge-sized hope she'd choose them over Otherside rose-topped cocoalots — and went outside in a snit to feed the frogs.

Of course, unlike every other witch in the universe, <u>SHE</u> does not keep frogs for the cauldron.

Oh no, not my Haggy Aggy. Since she decided to disallow all living creatures from our potions, she (or rather we, as I do all the work) keep them as PETS! And, as every frog in Wizton knows this, each night more sneak into our frog run trying to look like they've always been there.

I was busy shooing today's sneak-ins back into the woods when Bella leaped onto my hat. She started kissing me all over

(YUKKLE!)

and promising to do anything I asked of her if I'd let her come inside and watch TV with Haggy Aggy.

I was just saying,
NO — IF I LET YOU,
THEN ALL THE FROGS WILL WANT
TO COME AND WATCH TV TOO,
when HA started yelling "RB! Come
at once. You just have to see this!"
So, with Bella still clinging like
a frog-shaped leech, I went
back inside.

"This" was an Otherside Beauty Program and HA was bouncing about on the sofa screaming, "LOOK, RB! I can't believe it! It's such a lucky meeting of coincidences! They're giving that Othersider a makeover! AND THAT'S WHAT I NEED, RB — AND THAT'S WHAT I'M GOING TO GET — A TOTAL MAKEOVER. Do you know why? I'll tell you. SO I CAN BECOME AN OTHERSIDE SUPERMODEL AND BE ADMIRED ALL OVER THE UNIVERSE FOR MY BEAUTEOUSNESS!"

YIKES AND TRIPLE YIKES
was all I could think.

A witch — MY witch — wanting to be ADMIRED ALL OVER THE UNIVERSE FOR HER BEAUTY?

I shook my ears for webs and earwig nests. Was I hearing right? I was, because next she opened one of her new pink handbags and handed me a printed card picked up on her shopping spree. Here it is for your EDIFICATION:

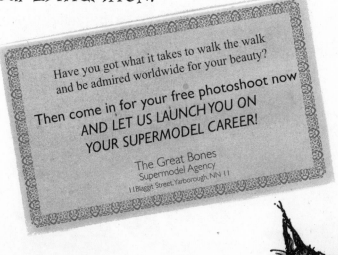

Have you got what it takes to walk the walk and be admired worldwide for your beauty?

Then come in for your free photoshoot now
AND LET US LAUNCH YOU ON
YOUR SUPERMODEL CAREER!

The Great Bones
Supermodel Agency
11 Blaggit Street, Yarborough, NN 11

"There. See," she said. "I overheard two Girls in Froth Accessories reading that and talking about it. As they were going along for their free photoshoots, I followed them. And for your information, in case you are wondering, a FREE PHOTOSHOOT is when they capture any number of pictures of you using motor eyes with motor memory."

At this, Bella (the Clinger, sliming up as usual) hopped onto HA's shoulder and started to yukkle her. "And so," she croaked, "did you get to be supermodelly? I'm sure you diddly did, being you are alreadily beauteous."

(Said so slurpily I thought I was going to stomach launch.)

"Unfortunately," HA pouted, stroking Bella with her spelling finger, "they turned me away before we got started. They snickwittered between themselves and then one of them said I should go and get myself a makeover and come back another day."

"Ribbitt, ribbitt, NO!"
slurped Bella.
"Not nice photoshootles."

"Maybe," said HA, taking a mirror from another of the new pink handbags, "but nonetheless RIGHT. Just look at me. Do I look like a supermodel to be admired worldwide for my beauteousness? NO! I look like a witch!"

At that point, she went on to tell us that she didn't know what a "makeover" was. But — having seen the

"TOTAL MAKEOVER SHOW"

on TV, now she does. (And so do I. Because she made me sit there and watch THE WHOLE THING.) And that's why she's so excited.

As a result, dear Diary, she's told me to drop EVERYTHING and find her the best makeover artist in the galaxy by the time she wakes up from a beauty nap!

Anyway, got to fly, as I'm meeting Grimey in the Deep Ditch for a catnip-ade. Maybe he'll have some ideas on the whereabouts of tip-of-tree-top makeover artists. He has ideas about most things, does my friend Grimey.

So, whiskers crossed!

Dear Diary,

Just got back from the Deep Ditch and thankfully HA is still in nap land. (With — can you believe this? — Cling-a-long lying on her pillow!!!)

I must say, as I always do, Grimey is not my best friend for nothing. First he cheered me up by telling me about his witch's plans for Fright Night. She and he are only going as *Inside-Outers!!*

Scary or what???

His Witch (Witch Understairs, a proper witch if ever there was one) has invented a spell especially for the occasion. He gave me a copy. Here it is. If Grimey just knew how lucky he is.

WITCH UNDERSTAIRS'S INSIDE-OUT SPELL

Wearing a hat five sizes too big, chant the following,
waving a fresh willow branch over and shaking an
admixture of dried ground slug slime and finely
crushed fossil shell upon the One to Be Spelled.

To you who for a day or night
Would be a horror-filling sight
On hearing this your flesh will hide
And take its Outside Self inside
While to your surface shining bright
Will come these bones — alive and white . . .
The skull, the ribs, the scapula
The clavicle and fibula
The phalanges — all twenty-six —
The stirrup bones like tiny sticks
The femur, that's the longest one
The humerus, oh yes, what fun
The elbow, radius, and wrist
And that's not all upon the list . . .

The pelvis, sacrum, tibia, knee
Patella and the vertebrae
Maxilla and the mandible
That lets us eat and have our fill,
The tarsals and the meta-t's
The ulna, carpal, what a wheeze
And since it is you're Inside Out
Your inner thoughts come hang about
Like elvish folk and tad-size trolls
Upon your outside bones they stroll
Your likes and hates, your hopes and fears
The ugly thoughts you've had for years
Now show themselves so all can see
The Inner Horror that you be!

Small print: This spell only works on those expressly willing,
for whatever terrifying purposes, to turn themselves inside out.

When we'd admired the chill and
wit-snatching factors of the spell, I told
him about HA's latest unwitchlike longing to
have a makeover and become admired for
her supermodel beauteousness.

"I mean, I ask you," I said. "If she wanted
to be admired for her whiskers and wart
count, I'd UNDERSTAND. I'd be right
behind her. I'd find her the best
wart-wizard around and GIVE her some of
my OWN whiskers. BUT BEAUTEOUSNESS??
And, another thing, what if the Hags
get wind of this?"

"They mustn't," said Grimey. "Under any happenstance. The High Hags would not consider the pursuit of beauty to be the practice of a willing witch. And they'll only blame you for not stopping it."

"They will," I said. "As usual. And all this on the day of the night before Fright Night? I don't know, Grimey, is she trying to RUIN MY LIFE?"

Grimey sighed, sympathizing with my precarious position.

"Even so," he said, "your first duty is to obey her whim and word. So if she's told you to find her the greatest makeover artist in the galaxy by the time she wakes up from her nap, then that's what you must do.

And I'll help."

After following a few ideas, all destined for shallow graves, we arrived at this supernova notion:

GRIMEY IS GOING TO DO

THE MAKEOVER!!!

As I write, he is spelling himself into the guise of Mr. Betelgeuse,

Traveling Makeover Artist

from and to the Stars.

But here is the nubbit and real brilliance of our plan.

He is going to "make her over" using his witch's INSIDE-OUT SPELL — without HA realizing, of course. This way, when she goes back for another free photoshoot, the photoshooters will be scared witless at the horrifying sight of her and, hopefully, run for their lives — stampeding all over their motor eyes and smashing them to unusable smithereens as they go!!

And that'll be the end of my witch being hotshot and made into a supermodel before anyone gets wind of it.

And still with time for us to get to

Fright Night!!

Cross my Lucky Whisker it works!

Meanwhile I'm off to spell all the mirrors in the house (see) so that when Haggy Aggy looks in them — after the makeover — she sees herself as the supermodel she wants to be and not the fur-curling, wit-snatching Inside-Outer

Grimey has made her over as!!

THROUGH-THE-AGES-LOOKING-GLASS SPELL:

Bind mirror with cobwebs and chant
the following while hopping on left leg,
right eye closed and right ear folded.

Mirror, mirror in my paw
Be what looking glass is for
Display each face that comes to you
To find if how they look will do
Reflect each one without the flaw
They think they have that closes doors,
SHOW THEM WHAT THEY WANT TO SEE
AND ONLY AS THEY WANT TO BE.

Small Print: If the mirror cracks, the spell has failed.

Even Later after It All Went Horribly Wrong

Dear Diary,

I'm sorry to have to tell you this. Our plan did not go according to itself at all. This was not Grimey's fault. He was a total moon and played his part to perfection.

No one could have guessed he was not Mr. Betelgeuse, Traveling Makeover Artist from and to the Stars.

Sitting there in top-to-toe pink in the "makeover chair," HA was completely taken in — even when Grimey/Mr. Betelgeuse insisted that she put a sponge plant in each ear (so she couldn't hear him chanting the spell).

All she kept saying was, "Do better than your best, Mr. Betelgeuse, and you won't be sorry!"

When the spell was done, Grimey and I stood waiting for the Inner HA to come to the surface and the Outer to take its walk inside. But guess what?

NOTHING HAPPENED.
NOTHING AT ALL.

I'm embarrassed to tell you but here it is: We'd forgotten to do the very thing every Familiar is taught to do in First Grade!

WE HADN'T READ THE SPELL'S SMALL PRINT — the small print that said . . .

This spell only works on those expressly willing,
for whatever terrifying purposes, to turn themselves inside out.

So, OF COURSE, it hadn't worked.

Haggy Aggy was not "expressly willing" to look like an Inside-Outer. Quite the opposite. She was "expressly willing" to look like a made-over worldwide supermodel.

Meanwhile, before we'd realized our
MISTAKE,
she ran around checking herself in all the
mirrors in the house and — since they were
spelled — screaming with delight.

UNTIL — and this is the stinky
sulphurous bog of it — UNTIL she made for
one of her new pink handbags and

PULLED OUT A MIRROR
I DIDN'T EVEN KNOW WAS THERE
AND SO
HADN'T SPELLED!!

Of course, in this mirror she saw herself as she really was and is: the least witch-looking witch in witchdom but still a witch — and the SAME witch in every way who had already been turned down by the Great Bones Photoshooters — and not in any single way made over!!

Well, a full-on fit followed (which I always admire, whatever the happenstance) during which she called Mr. Betelgeuse terrible names lik "shameless charlatan" and me a "doddified dupepaw" for engaging him. It lasted one hour and took five cups of comfrey tea and the rest of the rose cocoalots to get her out of it.

By that time, quite rightly, Grimey/Mr. Betelgeuse had vanished so it was up to me to come up with an explanation.

AND HERE'S THE THING, DEAR DIARY:

I DIDN'T HAVE ONE.

Luckily at that moment, the doorbell rang.

Tell you more when I can. Bella has fallen into a cauldron of spelled soup and HA is demanding I save her from the wild garlic.

Morning of No Nights to Fright Night

Dear Diary,

Be glad you are not me. Guess who was at the door yesterday saving me from one squelchy quagmire but plunging me into another?

Only Dame Amuletta, highest of the High Hags and clearly in a spreading mildew.

Luckily I saw her festering through the see-you-first-hole before I opened the door, so I bundled HA — still dressed like a Pink Powder Puff — out the back door and into the broomstick shed.

I pushed Miss Clingy after her with a strict instruction: "If you want to see another Halloween don't let my witch out of there until I give the say-so."

Then I dashed back and let in the Dame. It was worse than I thought. Far worse.

The cause of Amuletta's fester was HA's latest Otherside Shopalot Accounts.

She had them right there and was jabbing at them with her pointing talon.

"Converting what she's spent over there in this moon," she jabbed, glaring at me as if it was me who'd done the spending, "together with what she's spent in many moons previously, and not yet paid in kind for, she now owes the First Terrestrial Witches' Bank — namely us, the High Hags — 365 Spells, 215 Magic Potions and 95 Broomsticks."

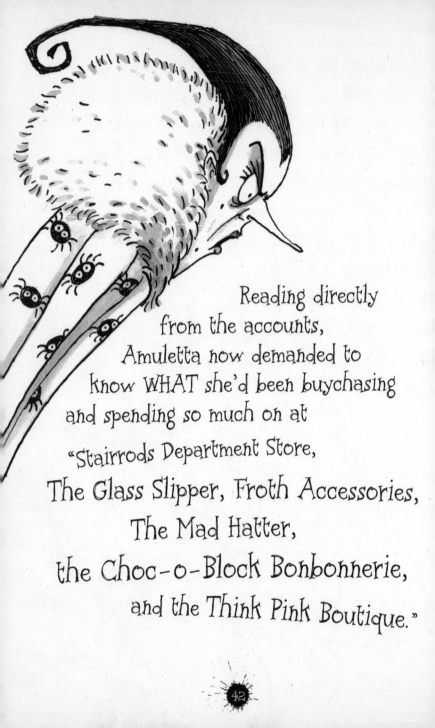

Reading directly
from the accounts,
Amuletta now demanded to
know WHAT she'd been buychasing
and spending so much on at

"Stairrods Department Store,

The Glass Slipper, Froth Accessories,

The Mad Hatter,

the Choc-o-Block Bonbonnerie,

and the Think Pink Boutique."

I was so cornered, I just burst out with the truth.

"PINK," I said.

"All pink, Your Hagship."

"I see," said the Dame. "And you, her trusted Familiar, allow this . . . this contraturvy buychasing of ALL PINK?"

I stared out the window — half hoping HA would burst out of the broomstick shed and come in

SO SHE
COULD ANSWER THE
QUESTION AND
EXPLAIN HER<u>SE</u>LF.

She didn't appear, and Amuletta was tapping impatiently.

"Well, Familiar Rumblewick? Do you have me an answer or do you wish to return to Awethunder's and relearn how to keep your witch OUT OF PINK and

OUT OF OWING THE BANK?"

I took a deep breath that infused my thoughts with enough fresh air to inspire them.

"It's a Fright Night thing, Your Hagship," I announced firmly. "I'd rather not say more and give away the thrill and wit-snatching factors, thereby spoiling the shock and surprise."

Amuletta was intrigued. She smacked her lips and shivered. "Ah, the thrill and chill of the wit-snatching factors. How I do love Fright Night. I'll look forward to this shocking pink surprise."

She shivered again and turned for the door.

I thought she was gone — but no.

"But where IS Hagatha?" She scowled. "Not invisible again? Such a tired old ruse when a Hag comes knocking."

"Broomstick shed," I said. "Can't be disturbed. Also part of the shocking PINK THING for Fright Night."

"I see." Amuletta pointed right between my eyes. "Well, Rumblewick, be that as it may. Quite aside from her pink buychases, she's now SO FAR OVER HER SHOPALOT LIMIT, she will have to pay the Pet Loan Penalty."

YIKES AND DOUBLE YIKES

was all I could think. The Pet Loan Penalty is when a witch has to loan a pet to the High Hags for one whole moon for them to use how they like!

And from what I have heard from pets who have been loaned this can include everything from scapegracing for the Hags' Familiars to spying on the Hags' ancient foes, the Space-Time Wizards, who use the spies they catch as space-boat ballast.

I tried to tell the Dame how badly HA needed me here.

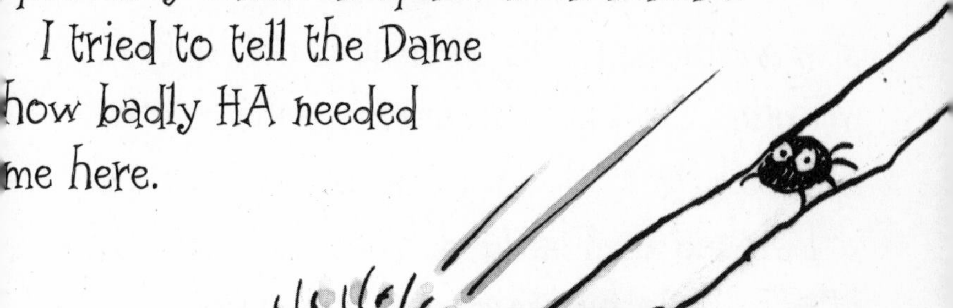

How she'd

NEVER MANAGE

FOR A TAD

OF TELL WITHOUT ME.

At which she cackled like a caught crawbird.

"And isn't that the whole point, you twitwickle creature. TO INCONVENIENCE HER? Teach her to keep out of Otherside shops and make her buychases here where she should on This Side at the Crafty Witches Co-Op where all our needs are catered for?"

I sighed and nodded.

"So hard wood," she snapped. "One Pet Loan it is and said pet will report to us at midnight, the midnight after Fright Night.

And, as far as I know,

THAT pet will be YOU!"

She swept out, slamming the door so hard
our thirteen chimneys rocked and rolled
their pots and HA came storming out of the
shed demanding to know what was going on
because the noise was frightening her
"darling little Bella."

Her "darling little Bella"?
Can you believe that?

While I was taking
the rap for her
shopping
sprees, my
witch had
been bonding
in the
broomstick
shed with
a frog!

After Midnight
the Midnight after Fright Night

Dear Diary,

It's been a madhare few days, which is why I haven't written. Still, you'll be glad to hear that somehow I've gotten my witch and myself out of the boiling cauldron and NOT into the fire.

But back to where I was — at the slamming out of Dame Amuletta and the bursting in of HA.

Apparently, while bonding in the shed, Mistress Cling-a-long had wheedled her way into HA's affections by suggesting the following:

That she should forget messing around with the shameless charlatans of this or any other world like Mr. Betelgeuse.

That if she is going to realize her ambitions of walking the walk and becoming admired universe-wide for her beauteousness she must get a

PROPER OTHERSIDE MAKEOVER LIKE THEY SHOWED ON THAT OTHERSIDE TV PROGRAM.

For that there is only one place to go, and that is at a proper makeover place on the Other Side like STAIRRODS Department Store.

(And from where, one has to wonder, does a mere FROG suddenly get such jumped-up ideas? I mean, I ask you. I doubt she's ever even sat on a sofa or seen an Otherside TV before she started wheedling her way into our lives and our house.)

Anyway — because of this clingy, yukkly, slime-up-to-my-witch frog's suggestions — I found myself tied in pink ribbons, wearing a collar bearing the Otherside name of Mr. Mog and flying HA — Froggy in her pocket — across the Horizon to the Beauty Counter of Stairrods Department Store!!

(AT LEAST I had the tell and the sense to pack a satchel to take with us — throwing in a few tried and tested spells, an extra hat and — just in case we were flying late — my now very impatient Fright Night costume.)

Arriving at the Beauty Counter (having left my broomstick in the Household Department for safe-hiding), I've hardly been **SO** embarrassed in all my lives.

HA swept in — demanding obeying.

"MAKEOVER, please!" she called. "As in the full kind. Like on that TV program. Why? Because I'm off to a free photoshoot. And better make it a GOOD one. Not like that Makeover Artist to the Red Dwarves, Mr. Betelgeuse."

She was bowed and scraped to and taken to a high stool. I was "told" (by her) to sit at her feet "like a good Mr. Mog" where I had to share space with an Otherside Unmentionable Doglet (belonging to an Othersider having her face decorated next to us).

From there — the floor — I could only watch in dismay as a Stairrods "Makeover Artist" covered my witch in all kinds of useless nonmagic potions! But if HA never gives up on her unnatural longings to be more Otherside than Our Side then I never give up in my efforts to stop her.

And so I got down to it.

While all the useless potion slapping-on
was occurring, I snuck behind the makeover
counter, found a pad of paper and
a writing tool, and wrote in my best
Otherside writing (which thankfully I'd
learned so well at school): DID YOU KNOW

YOU ARE MAKING-OVER A WITCH?

I pushed this in front of the
makeover Othersider.

She glanced at the page,
frowned, tore it off, and threw
it in her trash can.

I snuck back the pad of
paper and tried again.

I wrote: IF THE HIGH HAGS CATCH YOU THEY WILL HANG YOU OVER A HOT CAULDRON AND/OR SEND YOU BACK TO FIRST GRADE.

This message was also crumpled up and thrown away by the Makeover Artist — but I could see she was getting flustered. Mightily flustered.

So I took advantage of the fluster and went in with the big one, written in bright red crayonny stuff.

BE WARNED, I wrote,

SHE HAS NOTHING LEFT TO PAY YOU FOR WHAT YOU ARE DOING. AND SHE HAS

A FROG IN HER POCKET.

Well, that certainly did the trick, dear Diary — especially as, at that tad of tell, Bella popped her head out of HA's pocket and went, "Ribbit" — which made the Makeover Artist drop everything and

throw a screaming fit almost as good as a witch's.

But, by this time, HA was as good as made over and not about to hang around.

"Give her a spell for her work, RB, and get us out of here," she whispered as all kinds of Othersiders came running.

I grabbed a spell from my satchel (lucky I'd brought some), left it on the counter, and raced across to rescue our broom. Using all my obstacle-avoidance skills, I flew back through the store, picked up HA, and had us out of there in almost less time than it takes to tell of it.

My spirit
soared with our
zoom — just to
be away from
Stairrods — but
not for long.

HA insisted
we land on
a rooftop so she could
get her bearings for Blaggitt
Street and the Great Bones
Supermodel Agency. She was going to
the photoshoot and there was
nothing I could do to stop her.

Dear Diary,

Sorry — had to break off. A few witches and their Familiars dropped by to congratulate us — but I won't get ahead of the story.

So . . . we arrived at Great Bones.

HA told me to hide our broomstick and satchel in the courtyard outside.

She flounced in, me in her arms (having told Bella to keep down in her pocket).

And this time there was no turning her away.

They — the free photoshooters — fell all over her.

They seemed to like it when she told
them what to do as if she'd been photoshot
all of her lives: "Capture me here, capture
me there! Like this! And this!"

She posed, she flounced, she sprawled,
she kicked, she leaped in the
air. I can't remember when
I've seen HA quite so
"blown away" — and not
just by the windy hair
machine they produced
for her.

FLASH,
CLICK,
CLICKETTY CLICK,

went their motor eyes
with motor memory.

"FANTASTIC," they cried.

"YOU'RE A NATURAL."

"YOU'RE GOING TO FLY."

And that was when it all went
terribly wrong for her.

She was so carried away with the wind in her hair and their admiration, she forgot not to be what she is. "What do you mean, going to fly?" she cried. "I already fly! Would you like to capture a picture of that?"

They looked surprised but said they would — VERY MUCH.

"Then so you shall," she said.

"RB — I mean, Mr. Mog — bring me my means of flight."

But, outside in the courtyard, I found that my Giant Witch-Eating Tarantula costume had had enough of waiting for Fright Night, squashed into a satchel.

It had struggled out and was waiting to pounce — on anyone it could costume — and it got me.

So when I returned to give HA our broomstick, that's what I was — a Giant Witch-Eating Tarantula.

And the scene I'd imagined at the photoshoot if HA had been spelled INSIDE OUT by Grimey — now happened!!

The photoshooters took one look at me, at the broomstick I held in giant tarantula legs, at HA's face when she saw me and the broomstick (and realized what she'd done even asking for it) — AND WERE

TERRIFIED OUT OF THEIR WITS.

The stampede — to get
as far away from us as
they could — began.

We didn't wait to see where they went. We dashed outside ourselves and took off — me flying — while HA sobbed on the back of the broom at her own stupification for forgetting Othersiders don't do broomsticks. (At least, and for once, she wasn't blaming me.)

Of course, I now had only one thought in my head, which was: there's still time to get to Fright Night. So drop her off at home — since she doesn't want to go — and get there myself before the fun is over!

But soon after we'd
crossed the Horizon, who
should come straight across our
flight path but the High Hags.
"See you in the Narrow Avoid,
Hagatha dear," Clover Froggspittal called.

HA waved back while hissing hard at me:
"What have you done, nearly flying into the
Hags like that? Now they're expecting me,
so I'll have to go to this fright-full party
after all! And look at me. I'm hardly
dressed for it!"

Well, how wrong could she have been?
From the moment we landed in the
Narrow Avoid, it became clear to me we
were a sensation. Everyone who glanced in
our direction was so horrified they turned
into wobbling, dribbling, jibbling,
spineless blobs of
witless jellyspawn.

Later we heard the reason for this was that everyone thought HA actually was a REAL Othersider, in top-to-toe pink, actually infiltrating Fright Night with her Giant Witch-Eating Tarantula (me).

And obviously — as when all's well with the world, Othersiders cannot cross the Horizon Line — nothing could be scarier or more wit-snatching than that!

So, dear Diary, guess who did win first prize at Fright Night?

We did — my witch and I. (The Cling-a-long is trying to claim she played a part, but I say folderol to that.)

And so what has a place on our cauldron shelf? Nothing less than The Fright Night Winners' Trophy itself!

And one other supernova thing has happened: it suddenly dawned on me as we were flying home with our trophy, that

the "pet" in the Pet Loan Penalty

didn't have to be ME.

Hadn't Mistress Cling-a-long promised to do anything I asked of her in return for being allowed to watch TV/practically move in with us? SHE HAD.

So I sent HER along to the Bank at midnight last night to be loaned to the Hags for one whole moon.

Perfect, if I do say so myself.

As for HA — when we got home from Fright Night, she kept moaning and groaning and pointing at herself in the bathroom mirror and saying terrible things about herself like: "Just look at you, you silly starlight-loving twitwickle. From getting carried away with your own supernova-ishness and offering

to show how you can fly you've

robbed yourself of the chance to be

admired worldwide
for your
beauteousness."

In the end I had to warn her that
I JUST COULDN'T LISTEN
TO ALL THAT POINTLESS
SELF-BLAMING
A TAD OF TELL LONGER.

And if she didn't stop I'd have to put on
my hat and cloak and go down to the Deep
Ditch for a catnip-ade — and stay there
until she did.

"And anyway," I said, to comfort her,
"your makeover wasn't wasted. You looked
so like a beauteous Otherside supermodel,
everyone believed that's what you were
and we WON
Fright Night!"

And I think that did cheer her up because, right now, she's outside showing our Trophy to the frogs. And — music to my ears — I can hear her cackling uncontrollably,

for the FIRST TIME

IN MANY

MOONS!

Some of HA's pink shopping-spree bills and Shopalaot Accounts. Check them out and FAINT. I nearly did when Amuletta showed me.

FROTH
Accessories

Sparkly things	37.45
Spangly stuff	22.47
Jangly stuff	21.39
Jingly things	32.20
Hair stuff	45.01
Bags for stuff	38.23
Rings & Things	19.98

TOTAL: 216.73

Thank you for supporting our company policy which is:
"Throwing money away on Froth is good for you."

STAIRRODS
THE DEPARTMENT STORE

****

Lingerie	137.45
Hosiery	42.47
Tops & Bottoms	421.39
Coats & Jackets	232.20

SALE
Goods

TOTAL: 833.51

CUSTOMER COPY

100-200 GORGEOUS PLACE. SW22 1NE

The Mad Hatter
19 Noggin Square EW by SE

****

Many hats to
madam's liking
in one shade of pink
or another

400.32

TOTAL: 400.32

THANK YOU
for your invaluable patronage

The Glass
SLIPPER

1 pr style Twinkletoes:
pink   93.47

1 pr satin slippers:
pink   330.22

2 prs boots:
col pink   54.20

1 pr moccasins:
pink   115.00

1 pr style Ginger Rogers:
pink

TOTAL: 682.34

First Terrestrial
Witches' Bank

WITCH HAGATHA AGATHA
Thirteen Chimneys
Wizton-under-Wold
This Side
Bird's Eye View: 331 N by WW

Shopalot card number:
1313 1133 1331 1317

Cardholder:
Witch Hagatha Agatha
(Haggy Aggy or HA for short)

Pay In Kind (PIK) Limit:
350 Spells
200 Magic Potions
75 Broomsticks

SUMMARY	9 Notoctober Again	
Balance Brought Forward from previous moon's spending		320 SPELLS 193 POTIONS 70 BROOMSTICKS
Payments to your account in last moon		12 SPELLS
SPENDING ON YOUR ACCOUNT IN THE LAST MOON		+ 43 SPELLS + 22 POTIONS + 25 BROOMSTICKS
NEW BALANCE		365 SPELLS 215 MAGIC POTIONS 95 BROOMSTICKS
MINIMUM PAYMENT BY NEXT NEW MOON:		13 SPELLS 13 POTIONS 7 BROOMSTICKS

Ensure you get to the bank or send your Familiar in good time to
bring your Payments In Kind. Late PIKS, dud spells and potions,
unserviced broomsticks, and uncooperative pets will be charged
at our especially mean rate of 13 broomsticks each.

WITCH HAGATHA AGATHA
Thirteen Chimneys
Wizton-under-Wold
This Side
Bird's Eye View: 331 N by WW

Black Day the 4th – Washday 5 Notoctober Again

Transaction Date	Description	Amount
Last New Moon	Payment Received	12 SPELLS
Shrewsday 6th	STAIRRODS Dept Store	19 SPELLS
Shrewsday 6th	THINK PINK Boutique	13 BROOMSTICKS
Shrewsday 6th	THE MAD HATTER	17 POTIONS
Shrewsday 6th	CHOC-O-BLOCK BONBONNERIE	5 POTIONS
Shrewsday 6th	FROTH Accessories	15 SPELLS
Shrewsday 6th	THE GLASS SLIPPER	12 BROOMSTICKS

Day Before Full Moon Day Interest

11 SPELLS
3 BROOMSTICKS

Penalty for Dud Spell in last moon's payment

13 BROOMSTICKS

SUMMARY
We can't be bothered to do the sums, but at a glance you are over your PIK limit AND WILL BE REQUIRED TO LOAN A PET TO THE BANK FOR 1 (ONE) WHOLE MOON or pay any penalty we decide on any old whim.

WITCHES' CHARTER
OF GOOD PRACTICE

1. Scare at least one child on the **Other Side** into his or her wits — every day (excellent), once in seven days (good), once a moon (average), once in two moons (bad), once in a blue moon (failed).

2. Identify any fully grown **Othersiders** who were not properly scared into their wits as children and **DO IT NOW**. (It is never too late for a grown Othersider to come to his or her senses.)

3. Invent a new spell useful for every purpose and every occasion in the **Witches' Calendar**. Ensure that you or your Familiar commits it to a spell book before it is lost to the Realms of Forgetfulness forever.

4. Keep a proper witch's house at all times — filled with dust and spiders' webs, mold, and earwigs' underthings; and ensure that the jars on your kitchen shelves are always alive with good spell ingredients.

5. Cackle a lot. Cackling can be heard far and wide and serves many purposes such as (i) alerting others to your terrifying presence and (ii) sounding hideous and thereby comforting to your fellow witches.

6. Make sure your Familiar keeps your means of proper travel (broomsticks) in good repair and that one, either, or both of you exercise them regularly.

7. Never fail to present yourself anywhere and everywhere in full witch's uniform (i.e., black everything and no ribbons upon your hat ever). Sleeping in uniform is recommended as a means of saving dressing time.

8. Keep your Familiar happy with a good supply of comfrey tea and slime buns. Remember, behind every great witch is a well-fed Familiar.

9. At all times acknowledge the authority of your local High Hags. As their eyes can move 360 degrees and they know everything there is to know, it is always in your interests to make their wishes your commands.

Dear little ratlets (children),

Can't get enough of my brilliant diaries? Well, you're in luck! Simply turn the page for a **SNEAK PEEK** at my next few adventures.

AND, now that I've become star-spangled enough to have my own website, you can visit it at www.rumblewick.com and **VOTE** for which story you'd like to read next!

Most sincerely,

Rumblewick Spellwacker Mortimer B.

My Unwilling Witch
Skates on Thin Ice

It was, what seemed to me, a frozen-over boglet, its solid ice giving off a wispy mist. On the ice were Othersiders of all ages, shapes and sizes, gliding, turning, circling, running, dancing — and here's the thing, Diary — they were doing it on

KNIFE BLADES!!!

While HA gasped and clasped and unclasped her hands — as she does when her 'horizon expands' and she gets excited — I made my observations.

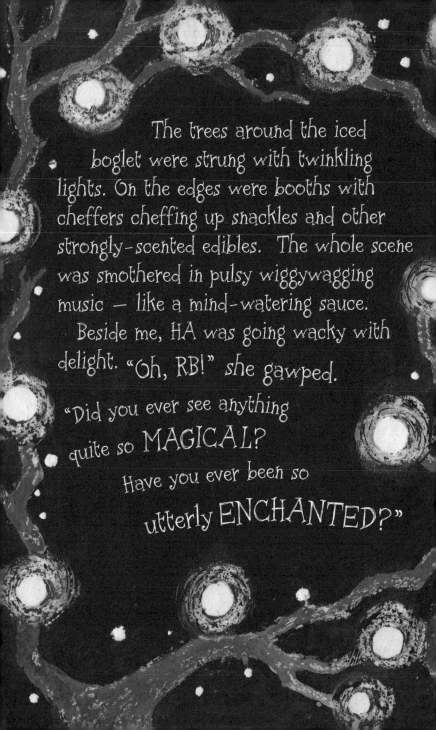

The trees around the iced boglet were strung with twinkling lights. On the edges were booths with cheffers cheffing up snackles and other strongly-scented edibles. The whole scene was smothered in pulsy wiggywagging music — like a mind-watering sauce.

Beside me, HA was going wacky with delight. "Oh, RB!" she gawped.

"Did you ever see anything quite so MAGICAL?

Have you ever been so utterly ENCHANTED?"

Whether I had or hadn't, it didn't matter.

I knew from her tone, we were only one tiny tadpole of a step away from her joining in.

She quickly discovered they were selling the knife blades (set into boots and called skates) at a shop on the edge of the frozen boglet called a rink — together with everything else Othersiders might like to wear while frozen bog dancing.

My Unwilling Witch Starts a Fun Park

Dear Diary,

Before I go on, I must go back — to my first experience of a Fun Park. It was this in a snail shell: HA is RIGHT and she has made a true discovery:

CHILDREN DO LOVE TO BE SCARED.

In turn, I have made an observation of my own: SO DOES SHE.

While I stood by and watched (or peeped as I couldn't exactly look with both eyes open or I'd stomach launch), she went on every ride and roller coaster — not once or twice but AGAIN and AGAIN. And whose screaming with the pleasure of terror was the loudest? One guess.

Yes. HERS!!!

And THEN, dear Diary, she got bored.
Half way through the day she found
me — by this time enjoying the sunset-red
fish prize attraction.

(Well, I had to do something while I was
doing something else more important which
was watching a Grown Othersider who
seemed to me to be following us, as if he
suspected we might not be what we were
trying to pass ourselves off as — ordinary,
Fun Park-loving Othersiders!! Why, even
now, he was edging up so he could
eavesdrop on our conversation.)

"RB," HA cried (not noticing him in her excitement), "these rides are fantabulous but they could be even MORE fantabulous. I've been talking to some children and they agree. So for them, of course, because my primary purpose is to make children cluckhappy, that's what I'm going to do.

I'm going to SPELL a ride into a pleasuredome of terror as yet unscreamed at. Come and see."

HA decided she was starving hungry.

"I have to eat <u>NOW</u>,
            this tad of tell,"

she announced to the whole roof and those
staring out from some roof windows.
            And then, almost falling off
                  the edge, she
                        spotted where
                        she wanted
                        to eat.

It was on the street below and called

THE GLITZERIA.

The outside was painted black and blue
and covered in gold and silver stars like
the night sky.

HA went into raptures. "That's the eatery
for us, RB. A starry, starry place. Get out
our foldaway broomstick — we'll leave
the car here for convenience — and let us
be hunger-answering AT ONCE."

I tried to talk sense into her
as we flew.

I reminded her that witches
NEVER eat on the Other Side
as it is well known the
food is grubspit.

"Old witches' tales!"

is all she snapped.

And before I could think of anything else
to stop her, she'd landed us, folded our
broom, tucked me under her arm like
Othersiders do with their unmentionables
(doglets) and was teetering into

The Glitzeria on her

high white teeter

ACROSS

1. Witches wear black pointy _____.
2. Rumblewick's rival
3. Rumblewick's best friend
6. Rumblewick is this animal
9. They rule all
12. Haggy wants one of these so she can be famous.
13. Rumblewick's job
14. Bella is a _____.
15. The best Familiar ever
17. Rumblewick's favorite food
18. Haggy prefers this to riding her broomstick.

DOWN

1. Rumblewick's witch's first name
2. The color that witches should wear
4. RB is dressing up as a tarantula for this event.
5. Where humans live
7. Haggy's favorite color
8. Haggy's favorite store
10. What HA should be learning
11. How Rumblewick measures time
16. Haggy is a _____.

Dear Precious Children,

The Publisher asked me to say something about these Diaries.
(As I do not write Otherside very well, I have dictated it to
the Publisher's Familiar/assistant. If she has not written it
down right, let me know and I'll turn her into a fat pumpkin.)

This is my message: I went to a lot of trouble to steal these
Diaries for you. And the Publisher gave me a lot of shoes
in exchange. If you do not read them the Publisher may
want the shoes back. So please, for my sake — the only
witch in witchdom who isn't willing to scare you for her own
entertainment — ENJOY THEM ALL.
Yours ever,

Haggy Aggy

Your fantabulous shoe-loving friend,
Hagatha Agatha (Haggy Aggy for short, HA for shortest) xx

Rumblewick's DIARY — Unwilling My Witch Goes to Ballet School

Rumblewick's DIARY — Unwilling My Witch Sleeps Over

Rumblewick's DIARY — Unwilling My Witch Starts a Girl Band

Rumblewick's DIARY — Unwilling My Witch Gets a Makeover

Rumblewick's

Ultimate Girl Band Sweepstakes!

Do you want to be a in a girl band like Hagatha Agatha?
Don't let Rumblewick stand in your way!

ENTER FOR A CHANCE TO WIN THE FOLLOWING PRIZES

One (1) Grand Prize consisting of:

- 1 Xbox 360 gaming system;
- 1 *Rock Band* 2 video game;
- 1 copy of *My Unwilling Witch Goes to Ballet School*;
- 1 copy of *My Unwilling Witch Sleeps Over*;
- 1 copy of *My Unwilling Witch Starts a Girl Band*; and
- 1 copy of *My Unwilling Witch Gets a Makeover*

Ten (10) Runner-Up Prizes, each one consisting of:

- 1 copy of *My Unwilling Witch Goes to Ballet School*;
- 1 copy of *My Unwilling Witch Sleeps Over*;
- 1 copy of *My Unwilling Witch Starts a Girl Band*; and
- 1 copy of *My Unwilling Witch Gets a Makeover*.

**To enter, visit
www.rumblewick.com**